Grandma Bubba's Warm Shawl

Written and illustrated by :
Rijuta Ghate

Translated by :
Rama Hardeekar-Sakhadeo

JYOTSNA PRAKASHAN

Grandma Bubba's Warm Shawl - JP 437

Published by :
Milind L. Paranjape
Jyotsna Prakashan
'Dhavalgiri'
430-31 Shaniwar Peth
Pune 411030

Mumbai Office :
Mohan Building
162 J. Shankarsheth Marg
Girgaum, Mumbai 400004

First Edition : October 2016
Second Reprint : 2023

Printed by : Unique Offset
Narhegaon, Pune, 411041

Price Rs. 120/-

ISBN 978-81-7925-472-1

Grandma Bubba lived quite far away on a very high mountain.
She was always busy with one thing or the other,
from morning till night. Grandma Bubba had lots of sheep.
Their soft woolen coats made them look like fluffy balls of fur.

Grandma Bubba took great care
of her flock of sheep.

She gave them food on time,
and medicines when needed.

Grandma Bubba
loved her sheep dearly.

As the weather grew cold,
Grandma Bubba thought of knitting a shawl
for herself... a nice, bright red shawl...
she could tuck into it while sleeping...

Then Grandma Bubba sheared
all the wool off one of her sheep.

She carded the wool and then spun it on a spindle.

She put some beetroots in boiling water
and dipped the wool into it to colour it red.
Then she dried it and made balls of the wool.
She took out her needles and
just as she was starting to knit...

Her grandson came running to her.

"Grandma Bubbaaa! I want a sweater!
A bright red sweater!!"

Grandma Bubba's needles began to knit...
tuk tuk tuk tuk...

A nice red sweater was ready
in no time at all!

Grandma Bubba's grandson was so happy to see his new red sweater!

He gave Grandma Bubba a sweet little kiss on her cheeks. Her grandson's tight hug was so much warmer than any shawl for Grandma.

Grandma Bubba then thought,
'Let me make a green shawl this time.'

She sheared the wool off
from another sheep and carded it.
Then she spun the yarn on her spindle.

She put the wool in boiling water
with some spinach leaves.
The wool turned a nice green colour.

She then dried it, before making balls.

She was going to start knitting,
when suddenly...

Her granddaughter came bounding to her.

"Grandma Bubba, you know what?
I want a cap! A nice green cap..."

Grandma Bubba's needles went on knitting...
tuk tuk tuk tuk...

The green woolen cap was ready
in no time at all!

Grandma Bubba's granddaughter was
super excited to see her new cap.

She put it on her head and
danced round and round.

Grandma was so happy to see that
her granddaughter liked the warm,
green cap so much!

Now Grandma Bubba decided
to make a purple shawl.
So she sheared off the wool
from yet another sheep.
Then she carded it, spun it and
made a nice long yarn.

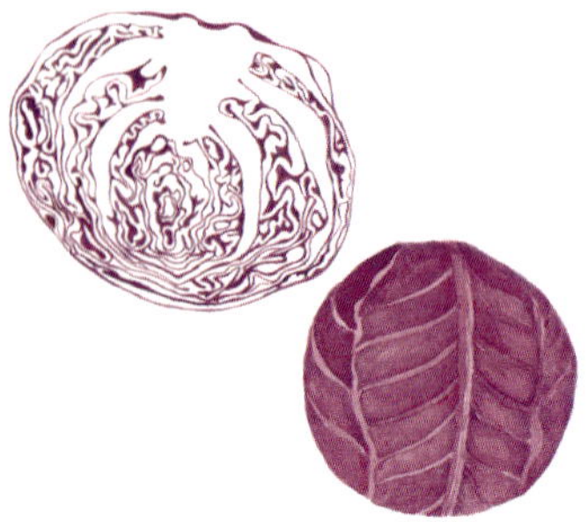

Grandma Bubba put a
purple cabbage in some boiling water
to colour the wool purple.
Then she dried it and made balls
from it. She took out her two needles
and just as she began to knit...

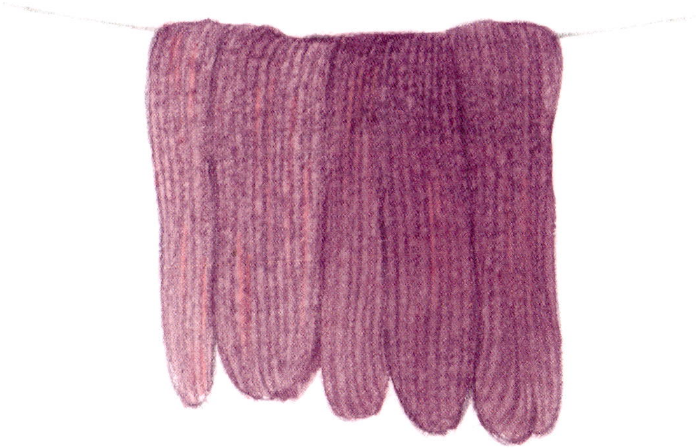

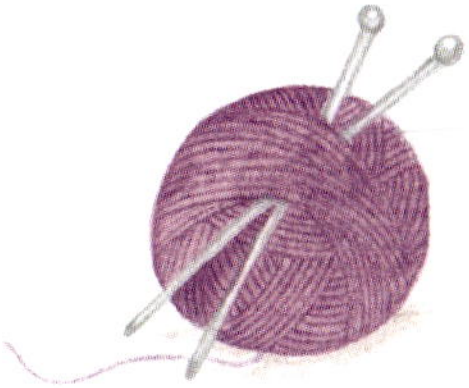

Her daughter-in-law came to her. "Mother Bubba, will you please knit a purple muffler for me?"

And Grandma Bubba's needles went
tuk tuk tuk tuk...

A beautiful purple muffler was soon completed!

"Oh, mother Bubba! You are so kind...
so lovingly did you make a muffler for me!"
Her daughter-in-law put the muffler
around her neck. She had tears in her eyes.
Grandma Bubba pulled her close in a hug.

‘Shall I knit a bright yellow shawl
this time?’ Grandma Bubba wondered.
Then she sheared the wool off
from another sheep and carded it.

Then by spinning it on her spindle,
she made a nice long yarn.

This time she put some turmeric in the boiling water to make the wool yellow.
She then dried it before making bright yellow balls of wool.

Just as she took out her needles to start knitting...

Her son came to her and said,
"Mother Bubba, my hands freeze when
I leave for work early in the morning.
Will you please make warm hand-gloves for me?"

"Why don't you use this yellow wool?"

Grandma Bubba's needles worked on...
tuk tuk tuk tuk...

A pair of beautiful yellow hand-gloves
was ready in no time.

Her son put them on immediately.
He hugged Grandma Bubba and
lovingly brushed his cheek on hers.

Grandma Bubba was very happy
to see her son in those yellow gloves!

She then thought,
'I will make a blue shawl now.'

Once again, she sheared the wool off
from yet another sheep and after carding it,
she spun a yarn on her spindle.

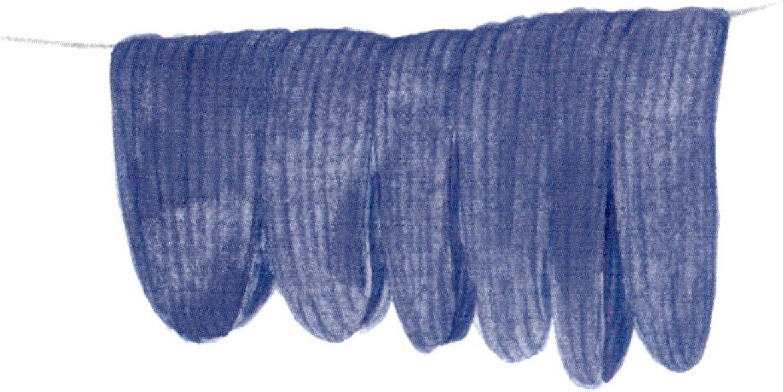

She put some indigo
in the boiling water and
dyed the wool blue.
After drying it,
she made balls from it.

She knew Grandpa loved blue.

'I must knit something for him as well.
What shall I make...?' she wondered.

Just then, Grandpa came grumbling to her.
He sat on the sofa pretending to be sulky and
said, "Huh! You made something
for everyone! Since so many days,
this cold is freezing my feet... why don't you
knit a pair of woolen socks for me?"

Grandma Bubba smiled secretly to herself. And her needles began to go tuk tuk tuk tuk...

Grandpa had an eye on her to see what she was doing.

And in no time, a pair of nice, warm woolen socks was ready!

Grandpa took the socks from her with a frown. But as the woolen socks warmed his feet instantly, he forgot to be sulky!

He pulled Grandma Bubba close to him and said, “Hmm... Much better now...”

Grandma Bubba saw that there were many colourful balls of wool left in her basket. So she started to knit a shawl for herself from the leftover wool.

Tuk tuk tuk tuk... her needles worked...

A nice big shawl was ready in no time! Grandma Bubba's love for her family could be seen in this colourful shawl. It was so beautiful!

Grandma Bubba was about to wrap it around her shoulders, when...

"Baa baa baa..." She heard bleating sounds...

Grandma Bubba went outside to see what had happened. The poor sheep were bleating in their fold. They didn't have wool on their bodies anymore to keep them warm. They were shivering with cold!

So Grandma Bubba lighted a fire outside their fold
and pulled them close to her. She patted and stroked their backs.
As the fire warmed them, they slowly stopped bleating.

Then Grandma Bubba put them back into their fold.
She brought thick grass matting from her house
and covered all the walls of the fold with it.

Grandma Bubba came inside. It was much colder now!
She served piping hot supper to everyone.
Then she told a story to her grandchildren to make them sleep.

She then climbed into her own bed and pulled the soft woolen shawl over her body. She slept a nice and sound sleep in the warmth of her new shawl.

Everyone loved Grandma Bubba's new soft, colourful shawl.